A DESIRE TO
WALK CLOSER
—— TO THE ——
HEART OF GOD

A DESIRE TO WALK CLOSER TO THE HEART OF GOD

(8) WEEK SERIES STUDY LESSION

PASTOR CHARLES E. YOUNG SR.

ISBN: 978-1-63950-210-3 (sc)
ISBN: 978-1-63950-209-7 (e)

Writers Apex

Gateway Towards Success

8063 MADISON AVE #1252
Indianapolis, IN 46227
+13176596889
www.writersapex.com

Our prayer is that this lesson will minister
to the whole man: Mind, Body, Soul and Spirit

Before starting this read daily 2 Peter 1:1-10

INTRODUCTION

The lesson's purpose and goal is to give those who are in Christ Jesus the tool's needed to develop in their lives the image and character of our Lord and savior Jesus Christ.

(Psalm 32:8) (Joshua 1:8)

There are four things needed to understand God's will.

1. Instruction

2. Wisdom

3. Knowledge

4. Understanding

Find the definitions of each word below

What is instruction

____

____

____

____

____

____

____

____

____

____

____

____

____

____

____

____

____

____

____

____

What is instruction

What is wisdom

What is knowledge

What is understanding

Read Proverbs 4:1-7

Which is the most powerful of the four

Which is the most powerful of the four

In order for us to walk close to God's heart we must first learn how to live holy.

Holiness is the key ring that the other key's are attached to, it is the Lord's command that we live holy.

Reference scripture on holy/holiness

Psalms 99: 1-9

Leviticus 20:7

Ephesians 1: 3, 4

Colossians 3:12

II Timothy 1: 7-9

I Peter 1: 15, 16

I Peter 2:1-9

Complete word definitions below

1. What is holiness

2. Holy means

____

____

____

____

____

____

____

____

____

____

____

____

____

____

____

____

____

____

____

____

____

3. Hallowed means

4. Consecrate means

____

____

____

____

____

____

____

____

____

____

____

____

____

____

____

____

____

____

____

____

____

____

(8) Lesson's/ Topics

1. Lesson #1 : Diligents

2. Lesson #2: Virtue

3. Lesson #3: Knowledge

4. Lesson #4: Temperance

5. Lesson #5: Patience

6. Lesson #6: Godliness

7. Lessons 7 & 8: Brotherly Kindness/Love

Diligence Definition and Lesson

Diligent: Giving persevering attention.

Persevering: To persist in anything taken.

To maintain a purpose in spite of difficulty

Diligence is an action demonstrated by what you do, to be willing to continue in the things of the Lord no matter what comes up against you to understand that nothing happens in our life without God's knowing and rewarding us whether good or evil.

Diligents endures afflictions and only surrenders to the will and word of God.

God's works agrees only with his word.

Reference Scriptures

1. Proverbs 4: 23

2. Proverbs 21:5

3. Proverbs 22:28

4. Hebrews 6: 10-11

5. 2 Peter 1: 4-10

6. 2 Peter 3:9-14

7. John 15:1-7

Seven Signs of Diligents

1. Diligents stands in the face of adversity and is unmovable.

2. Diligents sees the power of the holyspirit working for it's good.

3. Diligents is rooted in the word of God by faith.

4. Diligents is commited to seeing the end results of the Lord's promises.

5. Diligents doesn't complaint or faint.

6. Diligents holds fast to it's vows and doesn't waiver.

7. Diligents trust what the word of God says and holds to it's truth.

The Seven Signs of Diligents are the results of consistency.

There are three areas of consistency

    1. Consistency in study

    2. Consitency in our prayer life

    3. Consistency in our walk with the Lord.

How do you know when you have developed the character of diligents?

Answer: When you have set everything around your commitment to the Lord and no longer make excuses for not being available for his service.

Lesson #2 – Word Definition? Lesson of Virtue

Virtue: Moral Excellence, Power

Moral: Pertaining to or concerned with the principles or rules of right conduct, or the distinction between right and wrong.

Excellence: Surpassing or knowing when and how to make the right choice.

Power: Might, Strength and Authority to make the right decision.

Virtue is faith in action, it is the power given by God thru the Holy Spirit, that we may be able to endure all things that come upon us. To make the best of difficult or unsatisfactory situation. Knowing that if we abide in his word, he will see us thru. One thing know for sure sin will take virtue out of you.

Virtue will cause us to do (5) things

1. To be true, sincere, real

2. Be honest,

3. To be just, right, righteous

4. To be pure, genuine, true, simple

5. Of good report, kind

Scriptures References

Virtue

Luke 6:17-19

Luke 8:41-49

Phil 4: 5-9

1 Pet 2:9; 3:9

Power

Deut 8:18

PS 62:10-12

ISA 40: 25,26,28,29

Acts 1:8

Acts 4:1-7

1 Cor 2:5; 4:20

1 Tim 1:1-7

2 Pet 1: 1-3

Lesson #3 Knowledge

Knowledge: The acquaintance with facts, truth, or principles as from study or investigation. Knowledge deals with the facts before a decision is made, knowledge gives facts not opinion. It is the ability to understand, and apply information or instructions given to guide in all areas of life.

Reference Scriptures

1. 1 Kings 3:1-15

2. 2 Chronicles 1: 1-12

3. ECC 1:18

4. Proverbs 9:10

5. Hosea 4:1,6

6. Romans 10:1,2,3

7. Ephesians 1:17

8. 1 Timothy 2:1-6

9. 2 Peter 3:18

Knowledge gives/virtue/power to stay diligent and continue in holiness.

Temperance Definition and Lesson #4

Temperance is self-control, the ability to resist evil or the ability to exercise self-control, moderation or self-restraint in action or statement

Jn 14:26

____

____

____

____

____

____

____

____

____

____

____

____

____

____

____

____

____

____

Acts 24:24, 25

2 Pet 1:6

Patience Definition/ Lesson #5

Patience: Forbearance; Endurance

Forbearance: A refraining or holding back

Endurance: To abide, to bear up under suffering

Patience the ability given by the holy spirit to forbear or refraining from an action contrary to who you are; the ability to bear up under suffering.

Mat 18:23-31

Rom 5:1-3; 15:1-6

Lesson #6 Godliness

Definition: Godliness: To have faith to believe that all that takes place in my life as a a believer in the body of Christ, is to know that God's will is to build a quality of Godliness in my life which will develop seven character traits which will at all times cause me to have a reverent fear of God's presents.

The Seven character traits are as follow.

1. Knowledge: To know

2. Veneration: A feeling of awe, respect and reverence

3. Affection: Feelings, Passion (Good or Bad)

4. Dependence: The state of reling or needing someone or something for aid or support.

5. Submission: To yield or be subject to.

6. Gratitude: The quality of being grateful or thankful

7. Obedience: To submit, obey

Scripture

    1 Tim 2:1-3, 10
    1 Tim 3: 16
    1 Tim 4: 7,8
    1 Tim 6:6
    Titus 1:1
    2 Pet 3:9-11

Titus 2:1-8

Hebrews 12:1-3

James 5:10

Lesson #7/8

Brotherly kindness/ Brotherly love: Kindness to show grace and favor: The love of one as if to be a brother, a love indicating the closet fellowship as of man to man

John 15: 9,12,13,17

____

____

____

____

____

____

____

____

____

____

____

____

____

____

____

____

____

____

____

____

Romans 12:9,10

Romans 13:10

____

____

____

____

____

____

____

____

____

____

____

____

____

____

____

____

____

____

____

____

____

____

____

____

Gal 5:13,14,22

Hebrews 13:1

1 John 4:7-12; 16-21